Boom,

D1549469

Boom!

Coventry City Libraries
Schools' Library Service

CITY OF COVENTRY
SCHOOLS
LIBRARY
SERVICE
LIBRARIES

FOR NED – MM

FOR LAURIE – PM

HAMISH HAMILTON/PUFFIN

Published by the Penguin Group
Penguin Books Ltd, 27 Wrights Lane, London W8 5TZ, England
Penguin Putnam Inc., 375 Hudson Street, New York, New York 10014, USA
Penguin Books Australia Ltd, Ringwood, Victoria, Australia
Penguin Books Canada Ltd, 10 Alcorn Avenue, Toronto, Ontario, Canada M4V 3B2
Penguin Books (NZ) Ltd, 182–190 Wairau Road, Auckland 10, New Zealand

Penguin Books Ltd, Registered Offices: Harmondsworth, Middlesex, England

First published by Hamish Hamilton Ltd 1996
1 3 5 7 9 10 8 6 4 2

Published in Puffin Books 1998
1 3 5 7 9 10 8 6 4 2

Text copyright © Margaret Mahy, 1996
Illustrations copyright © Patricia MacCarthy, 1996

All rights reserved.
Without limiting the rights under copyright reserved above, no part of this publication may be reproduced,
stored in or introduced into a retrieval system, or transmitted, in any form or by any means (electronic, mechanical,
photocopying, recording or otherwise), without the prior written permission of both the copyright owner and the
above publisher of this book

Made and printed in Hong Kong by Imago Publishing Ltd

British Library Cataloguing in Publication Data
A CIP catalogue record for this book is available from the British Library

ISBN 0–241–13719–5 Hardback
ISBN 0–140–56091–2 Paperback

Margaret Mahy
Boom, Baby, Boom, Boom!

Illustrated by Patricia MacCarthy

PUFFIN BOOKS

"I've made a lovely lunch for you,"
Mum said, popping her baby
into the blue highchair.
"I hope you are
hungry, hungry, hungry!"

She did not know
that the animals
were listening
at the window.

"You have beautiful bread and honey.

You have two lettuce leaves.

You have a sweet apple, peeled and pipped.

You have a piece of cheese, and a raw carrot –
scrubbed clean.

What a lovely lunch for a hungry baby!

And while you eat it all up,

I'll just biddy-boom-boom on my
diddy-dum-drums. Beating those drums
makes me feel at ease with the world."

She did not know that the animals were
listening at the window.

And so Mum began to beat
on the drums.

BOOM-BIDDY-BOOM-BIDDY-
BOOM-BOOM-BOOM!

Closing her eyes, she smiled
as she listened to the beat.

She did not know
that the animals
were scrambling
for the door.

The baby looked at
her lovely lunch.
She picked up the
piece of cheese.
But she didn't eat it.
Instead, she threw
the cheese on to
the floor.

In crept the yellow cat – and ate it all up.

Boom-biddy-boom-biddy

MEW-MEW-MEW!

Then the baby picked up the bread and honey.
She leaned sideways in her blue highchair and threw
the bread and honey on to the floor.

In lollopped the brown dog with the ginger eyebrows –
and ate it all up.

Boom-biddy-boom-biddy   BOW-WOW-WOW!

Then the baby threw
the slices of sweet apple
on to the floor.

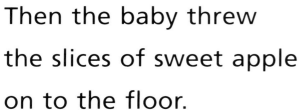

In scuttled the hens
and the red rooster
in their yellow stockings –
chuckling and cluckling –
and pecked it all up.

Boom-biddy-boom-biddy
COCK-
A-DOODLE-DOO!

Then the baby
threw the lettuce
on to the floor.

In trotted the black-faced sheep on her high-heeled hooves –
and ate it all up.
Boom-biddy-boom-biddy
BAA-BAA-BAA!

Then the baby
threw the raw carrot
on to the floor.
In ambled the
brown-and-white cow –
and ate it all up.

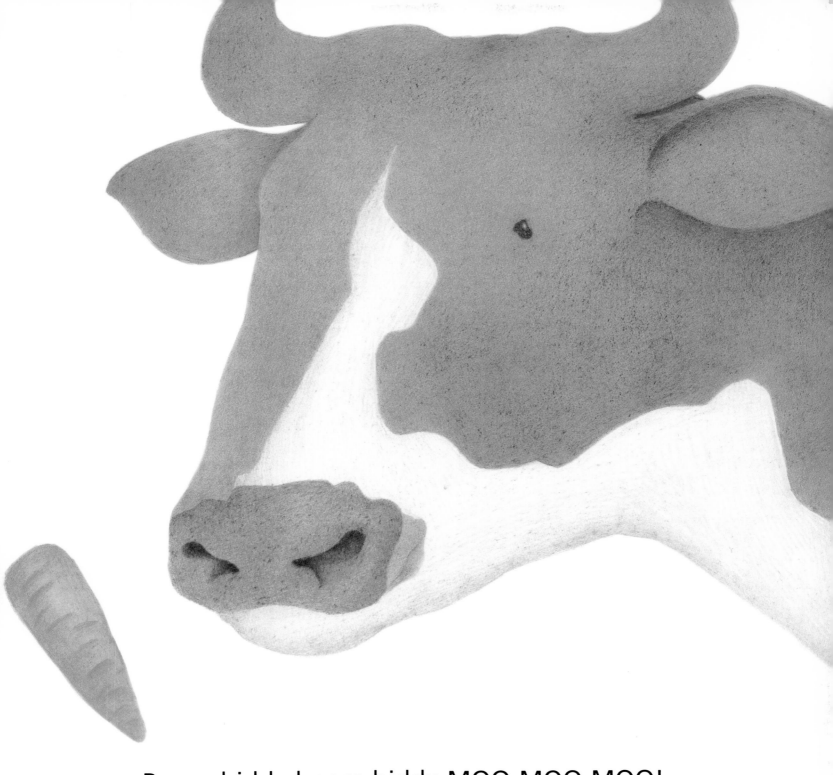

Boom-biddy-boom-biddy MOO-MOO-MOO!

Suddenly, Mum stopped
beating the
diddy-dum-drums.
There was no more
boom-biddy-boom-boom.

Out ran the cat!
Out ran the dog!

Mum sighed with happiness.
Beating those drums made her
feel really at ease with the world.

Out flew the hens
and the red rooster!
Out trotted the sheep!

Up stood Mum.
One last beat.

One last boom.
BOOM!

Out cantered the brown-and-white cow!

When Mum turned round,
the baby was sitting alone
in her highchair, waving
her spoon. Her plate
was completely empty.

"Oh, you good baby!" cried Mum. "You've eaten every bit and bite of your lunch. Listening to my boom-biddy-boom-boom beat must make you hungry, hungry, hungry!"

Then she hugged and kissed the baby and gave
her a banana – peeled and ready to eat.

And the baby ate it all up.
Boom-biddy-boom-biddy YUM-YUM-YUM!

3 8002 00748 6634

CITY OF COVENTRY
SCHOOLS
LIBRARY
SERVICE
LIBRARIES